P.D. HAYNIE

Unicorns & Other Monsters

Nine Medieval Fantasy Stories

Spiral Path

Publications

(Iteration 112019)

First edition

ISBN: 978-1-950237-07-4

This book was professionally typeset on Reedsy.
Find out more at reedsy.com

For everyone who has ever expressed faith in me as a writer.

Don't forget to tip the bus driver.

Contents

Preface

Shortly before my twentieth birthday, I allowed myself to become so freaked out by the future that was rushing at me that I came within fifteen minutes of jumping off of a tall building. I decided instead to make a run at being a novelist, and over the course of the next several decades I wrote fragments of a few novels and several short stories. I learned a great deal about telling stories along the way. I also learned that if you wanted to sell a short story, you needed to choose your market and target your writing. Since my personal muse is a recalcitrant layabout who only shows up a couple of times on a good year, that was never an option for me. When I had a story idea that needed to be extruded from my fingertips, it happened, even if no one in the world had any interest in that particular story at that moment.

In 2018, to the surprise of everyone who knows me, and most especially myself, I wrote a complete novel. I found myself with a sudden and unexpected need to learn to function in the white-noise ridden world of self-publishing. To that end, I pulled several stories out of my portfolio for the purpose of assembling a sample book. I learned a great deal, life was life, and I ended up publishing the novel, "Fiddler's Rose," first.

Once the novel was out, though, I had time to re-examine this little collection, and decided that it really deserved to see daylight. These are SOLID stories, and are well regarded by the scant bus load of people who have encountered them. They were written over a span of more than thirty years; the circumstances that brought each into existence are given at the end of each story. Two of them were written in a single day; one of them took four years to complete; another was rewritten several times over the course of a decade. They are all vaguely medieval. Purely by co-incidence, they are all written from the same third person omniscient point of view. It's a well balanced, cohesive collection, and I'm proud of it.

—P.D. Haynie

October, 2019

Valedictory

"Well?" the old man rasped. "What have you found?"

The healer was frowning; he shrugged. "It is the cancer. The lumps that you can feel are only the least part of it from what you've told me. The pains that you feel… imply that it is throughout your body."

"And?"

"The pain will grow worse; it will cripple you; you will die."

"How long?"

Again the healer shrugged. "Months. You, perhaps, are stubborn enough to live to see the new year. But I would advise you not to be stubborn. You have no need to further demonstrate your ability to endure pain, and stubbornness in this matter would serve no other purpose. You are faced with a fight you cannot win."

The old man chuckled. "It is my nature to fight, regardless. And I have been in battles I expected to lose before— such knowledge is irrelevant."

"It is also your nature to ignore all advice, regardless of its quality."

"Indeed." And the old man laughed.

==)»> «<(==

"Don't look so glum," the old man said. "You're going to greet the spring with a title, after all."

"How can you make jokes?" his son replied.

"It is my nature. I assure you, I take no pleasure in the thought of finally meeting Death as an invalid in bed— but it seems that I have no choice in the matter, and I will not mourn my own passing."

"It is an outrage! That you, of all people, should die in bed like an old woman. It is wrong!"

The old man smiled. "All these years I have expected to die in battle. But I have always been a little too good, or a little too lucky, or not quite foolhardy enough. And now, when I would relish the chance to be foolhardy, we are at peace. And next year will be too late. He has quite a sense of humor, has Death."

"And no sense of honor. I would gladly challenge him for visiting this indignity on our house."

The old man seated himself and looked at his son thoughtfully, then shook his head. "It is not your place to issue such a challenge; it is my place to speak, both for myself and my house. But I would be honored if you would act as my champion."

"What?"

"I hereby challenge Death to single combat for the indignity which he has visited on myself and my household, and I name my son and heir as my champion."

"And you expect Death to name a champion?"

"I do."

"And in the unlikely event that Death does provide a champion, you are actually going to allow someone else to fight your battle for you?"

"You misunderstand. I cannot fight on my own behalf— for I am Death's champion."

The son sat down suddenly, his mouth agape. "A duel between us? This is madness!"

"Is it? If you win, you will have spoiled Death's jest. And if you lose, Death will have us both. I think the stakes are acceptable."

"To the death, then?"

"How else? I do not think that Death's champion could either ask or grant quarter."

"I do not think I could kill you."

"Then you will have failed me and our house— and I really do not intend to give you a choice."

The son smiled briefly. "As you will, Sire. When and how?"

"Shall we make an occasion of it? A proper festival? We must at least have a farewell banquet. Noon, two weeks from today— bare blades and bare backs."

"As your second, I offer these terms to Death."

"And as Death's second, I accept them."

==)»> «<(==

The banquet was held, and was remarkably cheerful. The morning of the following day was another matter entirely; the knowledge that a close friend would be dead at noon preyed on the mind of every guest. Most agreed with the logic of the duel; all were glad that they were not in the place of either participant.

Noon came, and the combatants took their places. The challenge, the acceptance, and the terms were repeated for all to hear; the duel began.

The old man had been a master in his prime; even a year previously he had been beyond the measure of all but the very best. He was far from that now. But his mind was sharp, and his reflexes had not yet failed him; he lacked both the strength and the stamina for a powerful offense, but he was still quite capable of defending himself.

The son had difficulty making himself try to kill his father. He knew that he was the better warrior; he knew that he should have been in complete control of the combat— but he had no heart for it. He wished that it could simply be over.

They disengaged briefly. The old man said quietly, "You do your house no honor, Champion," and attacked. The son was caught off guard and was forced to block with his pommel; two of his left hand fingers fell to the sand. He stepped back, feinted, smashed the old man's guard out of the way, and sank his sword deep into the old man's side.

The old man knelt, then settled to a sitting position. He clenched his hand around his sword hilt and looked up at his son.

"Will you yield?" the son asked.

"In the name of Death, I yield," the old man replied. "I am well and fairly killed." And he released the hilt of his sword.

The son planted his own sword in the sand and knelt beside his father; he took the old man's hand. "From the day of my birth," he said, "I have loved you."

"And from the same day, I, you— and never more than this moment." They embraced, and the old man died.

And when my days are over,
Let me die with sword in hand;
Let me see my life's blood flowing
Into battle trodden sand.
Let me see my deathblow falling;
Let me feel it as it lands—
And my life's last friend
Will be the man
Who kills me
With his hands.

==)»> «<(==

March, 1984: This story was inspired by a conversation about "Star Trek: The Wrath of Khan", and was written in something like four hours ten days later. My point, during the conversation, was that the underlying theme of the film was aging and facing death, and that Kirk's wistfulness in the final scene was the result of his awareness that Spock had died well, a warrior's death, while it seemed all too likely that he himself would die in bed. My respondent was horrified...

Under the Wolf's Head

The orcs who had managed to take shelter in the woods had little trouble finding each other once the sun had set and they felt safe enough to move. The highest ranked of them— a platoon sergeant named Tagrath— did a fast head count and interrupted his usual torrent of casual profanity to swear sincerely. It didn't really matter how many of them were dead, of course; it would be all of them, soon enough. But the dung faces who were responsible deserved all of the curses he could throw at them while he was still alive to do it.

There were twenty-seven of them; twenty-seven out of one hundred and fifty-two— all that had managed to survive the ambush and the rout that followed it. They had gathered in a clearing in the center of the small wood without instructions, without any kind of plan, acting on a desire to be with their own kind on what was certain to be their last night. Tagrath wandered through the gathering, considering who was there and what condition they were in. He circled back to the best of the surviving scouts, who was slumped against a tree finishing off the last of his rations. Tagrath tapped him on the shoulder.

"Whitescar! Pick another worm and run the perimeter of this place— find out what the back stabbers have where, and particularly where their commander is, and if he's flying the Wolf's Head. Then get back here."

Whitescar looked up with disinterest. "Bugger off, Taggy. I'm a civilian."

Tagrath grabbed the smaller orc by the collar and hauled him to his feet with one hand; he used the other hand to press the point of a dagger against the scout's throat. "Dead civilian or live soldier, Maggot?"

"Soldier, Sergeant," Whitescar squeaked, and Tagrath dropped him; the smaller orc scuttled away on his mission before Tagrath could encourage him with a kick.

The other orcs saw the exchange, and realized that Tagrath was trying to restore military discipline. They weren't sure how to react to that; the Wolf's Head Company was dead, and no amount of play acting on Taggy's part was going to bring it back. On the other hand, just about anything was better than sitting and feeling sorry for themselves. Tagrath noticed the eyes on him, smiled, then took out his dagger and began to sharpen it. A few minutes later Whitescar returned and gave him the information he wanted.

"Listen up, Maggots!" he growled. "Anybody have any plans past noon tomorrow?" No one responded. "Just so there's no confusion— we're all dead. No one's going to get through the cordon tonight, and there are going to be archers all around before the sun comes up tomorrow, and they're going to set fire to this place, and we're all going to turn into orc cutlets, and there won't even be any officers around to eat 'em. Got it?"

There were grumbles all around; no one argued, but no one particularly wanted to agree. Tagrath waited until most of the murmurs had stopped. "I figure we have one other choice, one they haven't figured on. We're gonna die anyway, so why not go out in style?" Tagrath paused again, sweeping his eyes through the gathering to make sure they were with him.

"We stay here, we die like rats. We try to sneak out, we die like rats. We try to run, we die like rats." He paused again; he had them now. "But if we take back the Wolf's Head, and die defending it... We die like soldiers. And I'm willing to bet we can take enough of them with us to make sure they never forget the Wolf's Head Company. Who's in?"

There were no dissenters; Tagrath hadn't expected any. He drew his sword and started to sketch a map into the dirt. "All right... Here's the valley where they ambushed us yesterday, and here's this wood. About half of the bastards are out in the plain, east of here, making sure we don't head for open country. About half of what's left is here to the west, making sure we don't go back the way we came; the commander figures that's the way we're least likely to go— the safe passage he ignored doesn't apply at all if we go that way— so that's where he is, flying our standard as a trophy. The rest of 'em are along the cliffs, here and here, so we can't sneak out that way. Everybody with me so far?

"All right then, boys, here's what we're gonna do..."
==)»> «<(==

The humans rose before dawn, intent on being in position as soon as there was enough light to shoot. The units were still forming, getting ready to receive orders, when a group of orcs broke out of the east side of the woods. There was a brief skirmish, and then the orcs began to withdraw. The human assemblies started to break up; the soldiers didn't need orders to kill orcs who were already in their camp. The orcish sortie looked likely to be cut off short of the woods, but a volley of orcish arrows opened a path, and the surviving sortie members turned and ran. And the humans followed them.

The orcs charged down the path through the center of the woods, leaping cleanly over piles of debris that tripped and confused the humans, causing them to bunch into an ever larger pack. The orcs were nearly to the west side of the wood when a huge deadfall crashed down behind them, killing many of the fastest humans and blocking the trail. Another deadfall smashed into place behind the human hunters— and those who had not been crushed realized that they had been penned in, and the woods were beginning to burn.

Many of the humans billeted on the west side of the camp had rushed east at the sounds of battle, and a single volley of a dozen orcish arrows was enough to clear the way to the Wolf's Head standard. The human commander (who was above such minor tactical concerns) was still finishing his breakfast; Tagrath cut the man's throat with an expert flick of his sword: deep enough to sever the relevant blood vessels, not so deep as to risk getting entangled in the man's spine.

Tagrath hurled his shield into the face of an approaching human, wrapped his left arm around the staff of the standard, and grinned. "Time to die, boys," he shouted. "Make them pay for it!"

==)»> «<(==

Tagrath pulled his sword out of a fallen enemy and realized there was no one within reach of his blade. Dawn was only moments away, and he was surrounded by archers who were well out of his reach. He grinned again, and did his best to stand up straight. His sword was in his left hand; a wound in his right side had taken most of the strength from his right leg, and he was leaning on the flag staff with his right hand, using it as a crutch. He saw the archers relax, and wondered what that meant— and wondered if he could rush and kill one more of them before he died.

"Sergeant!" a voice bellowed; Tagrath turned to face the speaker, a human captain. "What is your name, Sergeant?"

"Tagrath."

"I command here, since you settled the colonel. I am prepared to accept your surrender."

Tagrath laughed and coughed up blood. "I don't think so."

"As you wish." The captain started to turn away, then hesitated. "I want you to know this was not my idea— to violate your safe passage."

Tagrath grinned. "Doesn't bring my boys back— or yours." Tagrath pulled himself closer to the flag staff; it was becoming difficult to stand. "Colonel Wormfood wanted to go on an orc hunt, and figured no one would care?" The captain nodded; Tagrath shrugged as well as he could. "Not the first time." He grinned again and coughed up more blood. "First time for me, though."

The captain held out his hand. "Forget surrendering, Sergeant— but if you will give me your standard, I will see that it does not fall." Tagrath stood his sword in the ground, then used both hands on the flagstaff to push himself upright; the captain gripped the staff firmly. "Do you want a grace stroke, Sergeant?"

Tagrath grinned a last time. "I don't think so." He stood to attention and drew his dagger, saluted the captain with dagger in hand, and cut his own throat as cleanly he had cut the colonel's.

The captain gathered his officers around him. "We'll dig a pit and bury them all right here— ours and theirs."

"You're going to bury the orcs, sir?"

"What did I say?"

"But they're orcs…"

"They were soldiers, and damn good ones. And another thing— no souvenirs. I want the orcs buried with their gear and their bodies intact."

"But sir…"

"Intact. No one takes swords or daggers or shields or bows; no one takes fingers or ears or scrotums. Intact."

"Sir, the men…"

"Any man who loots an orc body will lose a hand, and any man who desecrates an orc body will be killed."

"Yes, sir."

==)»> «<(==

When the humans marched off the next morning, there was a burial mound at the spot where Tagrath had died; the standard of the Wolf's Head company flew at its peak. Mounted at the top of the flag staff was the helmet of a certain arrogant human colonel; the same man's breastplate was secured to the base of the staff, and these words were engraved into the metal:

"At this place Sergeant Tagrath and the last remnants of the Wolf's Head Company killed twice their number and carried their standard into the afterlife. May it never fall."

==)»> «<(==

November, 1995: I like orcs. Or, at least, I like them when they are presented as a race that actually has some hope of surviving. This story took something like four years from the time the first line was written until it was finished. (There is a story in my archive that took SEVEN…) Several people have read this and asked for more stories about Tagrath, which has both flattered and baffled me. Tagrath was doomed from the moment of his conception, and is very dead at the end of the story. But I understand the affection for the character; I suffer from it myself.

Oasis

Gareth the Black looked at the map and scowled. The trap hadn't closed on him yet; he still had options. The problem was that whatever option he chose, it seemed he was likely to end up dead. He didn't like that, much.

Gareth had been leading a mixed band of goblins, gnolls, and orcs through the less occupied areas of the Kingdom for three years now, and had never managed to irritate anyone with enough power to deal with him until he had "kidnapped" the Duke of Argive's granddaughter. Of course, Cynthia of Argive had actually BEGGED to be kidnapped, and was likely to be killed along side of him, but that didn't really matter.

The thing that DID matter was that the Duke has dispatched 1500 men— two battalions of infantry, and a squadron of cavalry— to hunt him down. And now he had deep desert to the south, cavalry to the north, infantry to the east and the west, and perhaps a day and a half to live. He looked up at the faces of what passed for his officers. "Does anyone have any bright ideas?" he asked quietly.

The orc captain just rolled his eyes. He was an orc; orcs died in battle. He hadn't really PLANNED on dying this week, but he was ready. He was an orc.

The goblin captain shuffled his feet and cleared his throat. "I still think we would have a chance sneaking out here," he said, indicating a wooded area to the northeast.

Gareth shook his head. "Fifty goblins? Maybe. Fifty orcs? Probably not. All of us? No way in hell." He sighed. "I may give you leave to take your company and TRY, though, if I don't hear a better plan." This drew growls and worse from the gnolls and orcs, of course.

"Colonel?" the gnoll captain's second spoke up; he was a wizened and wiry old brigand who more than made up in guile what time had taken from him in martial prowess. He tapped the map with with a claw. "Redfang Oasis is right about here; we can probably make it in six days. If we hit this town here for supplies tonight, we could do it."

Gareth looked at the map, then at the gnoll, then at the gnoll's captain. SHE had just a hint of a gleam in her eye, Gareth thought for a moment, then said, "You're right. I had forgotten about Redfang. I think we can probably make it in five days, though, with about four more days on the other side to get back in the green." He turned to the goblin captain. "Rolgath? If you still want to try to do this by stealth, you're on your own." He looked them over once more, then said, "Right. Let's break camp, and get moving."

The gathering broke up; Gareth caught the gnoll captain's eye, and beckoned her to him. "Snark?" he said quietly, "Have a squad of your best hang back and put some time into obscuring our track; make them think that the goblins are the track to follow." Snark nodded, and Gareth continued. "And just to be clear? I DO know Redfang Oasis, so don't get any ideas about me. Right?" Snark smiled broadly, and nodded again.

Cynthia waited until the captains were out of earshot, and asked, "What is this about an oasis? Why isn't it on the map?"

Gareth shrugged. "It moves. Trust me; it will be there." Cynthia thought about that; her training as a sorceress had given her a fine sense of when

NOT to push a question, and she didn't.

==)»> «<(==

They raided the town just before midnight, and headed off into the desert some two hours later. Most of the orcs had been persuaded to abandon their metal armor, and had been encouraged to favor water rather than food in packing. "There will be plenty of both at the oasis," Gareth had said, "And you will want water more than you will want food on the march; trust me."

They camped at dawn on the south side of a hill, well out of sight of the town they had pillaged. They broke camp at sunset, marched through the night, then camped again. And again, and again, and again. As they made their sixth camp, Gareth told the captains that they should be to the oasis by the following morning, but that the troops should still be careful with their water. The orcs accepted the news stoically; the gnolls were guardedly jubilant.

Gareth crawled into the tent on the edge of the camp where Cynthia was already trying to sleep, got her attention, and put a finger to his lips. "This isn't a good morning to sleep," he said quietly. "Come and watch, but whatever you do, be quiet." And then he left the tent again. Cynthia crawled to the entrance of the tent, and looked over the camp.

The orcs had made camp normally, and were apparently already asleep; the gnolls had not, and were not. Their tents were half erected, as if they had been working on them only until the orcs were safely under cover, and then they had turned to making a number of odd structures out of spears: each structure consisted of two tripods, each holding either end of a crossbar some seven feet in the air. They reminded Cynthia of roasting spits, except that they were so high. Gareth sat down next to her, and she asked him what the strange things were.

"Draining racks, I think. We'll have to see."

Snipe, the grizzled gnoll lieutenant, ambled toward them. "We're about ready to begin the party, Colonel," he said. "With your permission."

Gareth shrugged. "I think I've already given it." Snipe smiled, saluted, and went back to the other gnolls.

"Gareth…" Cynthia suddenly needed to know what was happening, but didn't know how to frame the question. Gareth looked into her eyes, and shrugged again.

"No point in secrets now, I imagine," he said quietly. "Have you ever heard of ANYONE who has crossed this desert?"

"No…"

"I have. The only way to do it is pack heavy on water, light on food, and then kill and eat your pack animals as soon as you can consolidate the load away from one of them." Gareth paused, and Cynthia's eyes got wide as she realized what he was saying. "They're going to kill the orcs, steal their water, drain their blood for later, and eat their bodies. When we leave here, the gnolls will be well fed, and their packs will be full again."

Cynthia started to say something, but was silenced by the beginning of the gnoll ambush. Working in groups, the gnolls collapsed each orc tent in turn, pinning the occupants and stabbing them to death through the canvas; the slaughter was over in minutes, and the gnolls started to collect both water and empty waterskins. The dead orcs were hoisted onto the draining racks, their blood was collected, and the bodies were stacked into another pile for consumption or disposal.

Snipe ambled back to them. He was carrying a waterskin that bore stains to indicate it was full of something other than water. He offered it to Gareth. "It's bad luck to visit Redfang and not at least taste the fountain," he said with a smile. Gareth looked him in the eye, then accepted the skin and took a deep drink. "Lady Cynthia?" Snipe asked; she reacted in horror. This was NOT the life she had envisioned.

"Drink or be drunk, Cyn; it's their way," Gareth said softly. Cynthia stared at him in horror, but accepted the waterskin, and drank from it. Snipe smiled, saluted, and returned to the slaughter.

"I had no idea they were so VILE," Cynthia hissed when Snipe was out of earshot.

Gareth just shrugged. "Sure you did. And they're not really vile... they're just gnolls."

==)»> «<(==

February, 2006: I always liked gnolls, from the first time I encountered them in Dungeons & Dragons. But I assumed that they were purely an artifact of that game, and didn't otherwise think about them. In the late 1990s I developed an odd affinity for hyenas, and thought about gnolls a bit more, but still did nothing with them, because I thought of them as someone else's property. In 2006 I learned that gnolls had acknowledged literary antecedents, and were actually in the public domain, and suddenly I found them MUCH more interesting. Hyenas are giant weasels whose main taxonomic distinction is an ability to crush bones with their teeth; gnolls are anthropomorphic hyenas who enjoy eating other sentients. Both hyenas and gnolls are matriarchal. How can you NOT love these guys? (Also: This story bears a sideways dedication to Roald Amundsen. I leave it to the curious reader to figure out why.)

Minotaur

As the sun set, the minotaur almost emerged from cover at the edge of town and bellowed. The men of the town did not know better, so they armed themselves and gathered together and went off into the woods to hunt the creature that made the noise. The minotaur killed them, then entered the town and impregnated every woman who was not too old, too young, or already pregnant. No female who gets within five paces can resist the call of a minotaur; such is the nature of their magic.

At another town, the minotaur bellowed, and the people of the town, who were not utter fools, barricaded themselves in the strongest building in the town and prepared to defend themselves. Once it was completely dark, the minotaur broke in and killed all of the men, for any male who gets within five paces of a minotaur becomes paralyzed with fear; such is the nature of their magic. And THEN the minotaur impregnated all of the women who were not too old, too young, or already pregnant.

At a third town, the minotaur bellowed, and someone in the town knew what to do. The men of the town were persuaded to hide until dawn, and the women of the town were gathered in the town square. The minotaur then impregnated all of the women who were not too old, too young, or already pregnant. This was not ideal, but at least no one died.

At a fourth town, the minotaur bellowed. There was a hunter in the town, and at her insistence, the men of the town hid, and the women of the town gathered in the town square. The minotaur approached the women, and the hunter rose from among them and shot the minotaur in the throat with her crossbow. The minotaur fell, but did not die, and the hunter pinned it to the ground with a spear through the chest. Once the minotaur died, the hunter severed its head with an axe, and then sawed off the minotaur's horns, and told the people of the town to burn the other remains.

The hunter's job was not done. She back tracked the minotaur to every town he had visited, and she took an inventory of every woman that the minotaur had impregnated. There would be dozens of children, and she had to make sure of each of them. The vast majority of the children would be female, and they would be no problem. The hunter was one such herself, as was her mother. But the male children would need to be killed just as she had killed her own son, because the male children of minotaurs grew up to become minotaurs themselves; such is the nature of their magic.

==)»> «<(==

November, 2016: This is an effort to turn a (dark and depressing) piece of my personal mythology into a story. I am happy with it on that score. If nothing else, it illustrates that when you apply story structure to an information dump, you get a fable.

Unicorn Dagger

Once upon a time there was a unicorn who had lost his companion. This is not unusual; unicorns are long-lived, and the two legged kindreds are often fragile. The unicorn sought out a young sorceress and recruited her as his new companion, taught her the things he needed her to know, and the two of them had many adventures together.

It came to pass on one of these adventures that the unicorn was killed; this is not unusual, either, for while unicorns are long-lived, they are still mortal. The unicorn's companion managed, with some difficulty, to survive the circumstances of the unicorn's death, and, after some considerable effort, secured the unicorn's body. She removed the unicorn's horn— a task which can not be accomplished by brute force, but is easy for one who knew the unicorn in life, and knows the proper spell— and then burned the rest of the body. She took the horn and sought out a Master Sorcerer, for she did not have enough magic for the task she needed done.

Now, the horn of a unicorn is a wonderful thing. The material is stronger and more flexible than steel, harder than diamond, and resembles a marriage of ivory and opal. Of course, this means that it can not be worked by any normal tools, but there are alternatives. When a unicorn dies, its spirit takes up residence in the horn (or not, in which case the horn crumbles to dust, but that is another story) . So while the horn is not really alive, neither is it truly unliving, and certain spells which shape living flesh can be used, with the consent of the unicorn's spirit, to transform such a horn into something somewhat more useful than its natural shape. It was for just this reason that the unicorn's companion sought out a Master Sorcerer.

In due course, the sorceress found such a Master, terms were arranged and met, and the horn was shaped into a dagger. The dagger was simple and elegant, and the material made it so beautiful that the Master was reluctant to part with it, but the sorceress insisted that he honor his bargain, and then she went on her way.

The sorceress wandered the wide world, and had many more adventures. The spirit of the unicorn who had been her master was with her through all of them, keeping her young and healthy for decades, and aiding her with advice and with various magics which were intrinsic to the horn and ghost of a unicorn.

The Master Sorcerer, for his part, continued to study and thrive. He survived the transition to Grand Master with his sanity, but not his conscience, intact. Having the power to simply take anything he wanted without fear of reprisal pleased him a great deal. He decided he wanted a dragon bone staff, and killed a reclusive and otherwise harmless dragon to get it. And then he remembered the beautiful dagger he had shaped from the horn of a unicorn, and decided that he deserved to have it back, NEEDED to have it back. And so he began to plot to retrieve it. He sent thieves to steal the dagger, but they failed; he sent assassins to kill the sorceress and THEN steal the dagger, and they failed as well. Eventually, he grew bored and confronted the sorceress himself. He blasted her to ash and then he took the dagger home.

The unicorn ghost within the dagger was not pleased by this turn of events, but he lacked the power to resist a Grand Master Sorcerer, and was enslaved. But he was not without resources; he was clever, and devious, and he could charm the wet out of water.

The unicorn had many secrets, and the sorcerer could not force them into the open if he did not suspect that they existed. The sorcerer knew that the unicorn could heal, and converse with anyone who held the dagger, and could prevent aging. He did not know that the edge of the dagger was always exactly as sharp or as dull as the unicorn wished, or that the unicorn could pull the minds of dreamers, and other ghosts, into his private dreamworld. And the sorcerer most particularly did not know that unicorn could saddle any wound the dagger struck, no matter how small, with the magical force of his entire will.

The unicorn waited, and flattered, and lied, and hid. He also explored his surroundings to the best of his abilities, and found that the dragon spirit within the sorcerer's staff hated the sorcerer every bit as much as he did, which gave the unicorn a co-conspirator and confidant.

One day, inevitably, the sorcerer was careless with the dagger, and cut himself. It was a very small cut, and released a single drop of blood, a tiny drop, but it was enough. The unicorn's magic flared, and all of his rage and hatred and frustration poured into the sorcerer's body. The sorcerer's heart exploded, and he fell dead.

But Grand Master Sorcerers do not die easily, and he had made preparations. His spirit retreated into the dragon bone staff, from whence he could steal the body of anyone who had the misfortune to touch the staff. Or at least, that was the way he had planned it. He had not realized that, without the support of his living body, his spirit was not as strong as the spirit of the staff. And he had not realized that the spirit of the staff hated him with all of its draconic heart. And he had not counted on the unicorn.

The unicorn pulled the sorcerer, and the dragon, into his dreamworld, and unicorn and dragon conspired to make the sorcerer's existence as miserable as possible. The sorcerer learned that ghosts can feel pain, and fear, and above all, misery.The sorcerer had never been a brave man, and he found that he had no will to resist the scorn and hatred and torture of his former slaves. It did not take him long to simply give up, and will himself out of existence.

This left the dagger, and the staff, and the ghosts within them abandoned in the sorcerer's sanctum. But that was not so great a hardship; they knew that someday someone would find them, and in the meantime, the dragon was female and lonely, and the unicorn could charm the wet out of water.

==)»> «<(==

September, 2019: I have been living with lustful, charming, borderline sociopathic unicorns for about four decades, and with haunted unicorn horn daggers for about half that long. This particular story first saw daylight in 2009, and has been retold several times since. A friend who read the earliest version said it was the most bleak and depressing fable she had ever encountered, and I don't doubt it; it was grim. This version is not exactly happy, but happier, and better structured.

Those who have read my novel "Fiddler's Rose" will recognize Fiddler the unicorn, though this presentation does not exactly match the story as Fiddler tells it in the novel. There are two possible reasons for this. One is that the structural demands of a short story are different from those of a tale related conversationally within a novel, and the other is that,well, it's Fiddler, and his relationship with the truth is always a bit of a problem.

The Girl on the Hearth

Once upon a time there was a beautiful young parlor maid, who, through no fault of her own, came to the attention of her master's singularly handsome son. Nature took its course, and in due time the girl found that she was going to have a child.

The young man swore that he would do right by the girl, by which he meant that he would demote her from the parlor to the scullery, but allow her to remain employed; the girl had rather different hopes, but no one asked after them. The young man's father, on the other hand, insisted that the girl be thrown into the street at once, and the argument between father and son became so heated that the old man suffered a stroke and died. So the young man got his way.

The child was a girl, and she was named Ember for her hair. Some time after she was born, the young master married a woman appropriate to his social status, and some time after that, the couple produced a daughter, and then later, another daughter. And then Ember's mother died, and Ember was left to grow up with her two half sisters.

Ember was never allowed to forget that she was a servant, and a servant's daughter, but she was also allowed to take part in her half-sisters lessons if they did not interfere with her chores. Ember made very sure that her chores did not interfere; she was as eager a student as her half sisters were indifferent.

As the three girls came of age to be married, the old housekeeper died, and Ember took over as the senior female servant. And shortly after that, the girls' father was killed in a riding accident, leaving his wife with full control of his estate. Ember's life became very busy, and not very pleasant.

And then one day the word was spread that the King was sponsoring a festival in honor of the marriage of his daughter, which would include full state balls on three consecutive nights. It was also rumored that one of the goals of the festivities was to allow the King's heir to choose a bride from among all of the available noblewomen.

Ember found herself buried in the task of outfitting her stepsisters for the festival. She herself was a commoner, and not eligible to attend, but she did have an opportunity to examine all that was fashionable. And she decided exactly what she would wear, in every detail, if the opportunity to attend did arrive.

There was one other thing about Ember that no one in the household even suspected: she could talk to ghosts. Her mother's ghost was friendly, though of little use, but her grandmother's ghost knew many forbidden things, and her great-grandmother knew more still. And late at night, deep in the bowels of the house, Ember would learn all that she could from generations of dead witches. And they found her just as eager a pupil as any of her other teachers.

On the first night of the festival, after her step mother and half sisters had been safely shipped away, Ember went to the stable and climbed onto the back of an old plow horse, and rode him to the palace. And along the way she wove a glamour, so that by the time she arrived, she seemed to be riding in a huge and beautiful carriage drawn by four magnificent horses.

She stopped at the foot of the grand entryway, and a footman who wasn't there (though no one else knew that) helped her to the ground, and the carriage pulled away. No one questioned her right to attend, though no one knew who she was; only someone of the highest nobility could possibly dress with such a combination of elegance, taste, and fashion.

The prince was drawn to her as a moth to a flame; she danced with him, and she talked with him, and he marveled at her depth. And as soon as he (very reluctantly) allowed himself to be taken from her company, she vanished. Not literally, of course; she simply withdrew from sight for a moment, dropped the glamour, and then blended in with the royal servants to make her escape.

She repeated the performance the following night; she responded to the prince's questions about her name and origin by saying that it was a riddle, and surely he did not wish to give up so easily.

By the third night the prince was beside himself. He waited at the entrance for Ember to arrive; he would dance with no one but her; he could not get enough of her conversation. And then, as midnight approached, she prepared to take her leave. The prince tried to stop her, but she would not be dissuaded; she said that if she did not leave before midnight, the prince would never get the key to the riddle.

The prince followed her to her carriage and watched her climb in; as she did, she kicked off one of her shoes and left it in the road beside the carriage. She called to the prince that it was his key, and that when he found the shoe's mate, he would have solved the riddle.

For thirty days, the prince tried to find the matching shoe. No one knew who had made it; no one knew where it had come from. And certainly no one knew where the matching shoe was. As the days went by the prince became increasingly distraught; for a while he even experimented with having every woman he met try the shoe on, but even in his despair he soon recognized the madness of that.

On the thirtieth day following the ball, a withered old woman visited the prince and told him that she could solve the riddle if he was certain that he wanted the answer. The prince answered that of course he wanted the answer; he was in love with the girl; he would do anything to find her.

The old woman asked if the prince would marry her, and the prince said that that was his intention. The old woman asked if he were certain, if he would marry her even if she were a commoner. The prince swore that he would marry her as long as she were a human woman, and the old woman smiled.

The old woman then called to one of the prince's dogs, which came to her as if it knew her, and asked the prince for the shoe. She tied the shoe to the dog's collar, and said that the dog should be allowed to run free, but followed, and that it would reach its goal at noon on the next day. And then the old woman left.

At noon the next day, the dog led the prince to the house where Ember lived. Ember's stepmother was very surprised to see him, and even more surprised when he told her that he intended to marry one of the women of the house. Ember's half sisters were summoned, and dismissed, and then the servants were brought out; Ember carried with her a loaf of freshly baked bread.

Ember's stepmother protested that there must be some mistake, but the prince recognized Ember at once. The stepmother protested even more, and Ember tore open the loaf of bread to reveal the missing shoe.

Ember and the prince were married, and eventually became King and Queen, and Ember, at least, lived happily ever after. The prince was forever haunted by the knowledge that he would never again know when he was acting of his own free will, or merely dancing as Ember pulled his strings.

==)»> «<(==

February, 2000: Once upon a time, my wife and I were discussing fairy tales, and we fell into a comparative analysis of fairy tale romances. There is consistently a heroine, a lover, and an enemy, and there is magic. In "Sleeping Beauty", the enemy has the magic; in "Beauty and the Beast", the lover has the magic; in "Cinderella", the magic comes in out of left field, most recently in the form of the "Fairy God Mother", but in older versions of the tale as the ghost of the girl's mother. And I thought, "Well, that's lame; it's clear that this SHOULD be the third permutation, in which the girl herself has the magic." Cinderella has been told many, many times, with many variations, but never like this. Which is a shame, because this version of the story has been my absolute favorite from the moment I finished writing it.

Third Chance

Auntie Thistle had a small house in the woods an almost safe distance past the edge of town. She was a healer and a rustic apothecary, and she made the local men nervous. The local women liked her and trusted her, and everyone respected her. She had been old when she first came to town, and she had lived there for a very, very long time.

Sometimes, on summer nights when the moon was full and the sky was clear, the young women of the town would gather and travel as a gaggle to Auntie's house, and she would have a fire burning, and a cauldron of stew simmering, and the girls would eat and giggle and generally be girls until late into the evening. And Auntie Thistle would tell them stories.

On one such night, one of the girls made a comment about a unicorn, and Auntie rolled her eyes and said that it wasn't close to being true, and another girl asked Auntie if she knew any unicorns stories, and Auntie smiled and shrugged and said that she might. And the girls got quiet, and the circle formed, and Auntie started to tell her tale.

"A very, very long time ago," she began, "There was a girl named Amber who had a huge collection of silly ideas where her brain should have been." There were giggles from the gallery; Auntie continued, "She was much like several of you in that regard, I think. But Amber was also unlucky, and so she found herself expecting a child. There were no local boys of her own age who could be conscripted as the father, and the real father was a wanderer who was long gone, so Amber found herself married to a widower who was about three times her age." There were expressions of disgust and horror from the gallery; Auntie rolled her eyes, and waited for quiet.

"Amber didn't really have a bad life," Auntie continued. "But the life she had was so far from the life she had imagined, the life she wanted, that she was always unhappy, and usually angry. She hated pretty much everyone, except her son, Oak. Well, she hated him, too, but she also loved him, and that mitigated the hatred."

Auntie took a sip from the bottle that she never shared. "Time passed; Amber's husband died, and Oak grew to adulthood. He was a very adequate young man; he might have been more, had he not been so thoroughly buried in the shadow of his mother's anger."

"I thought this was a story about unicorns!" one of the girls mumbled; Auntie looked at her and said nothing, but the other girls quickly shushed the complainant.

"There was a girl in the town named Beryl. She was a bit younger than Oak, and she thought the sun rose and set on the boy. Oak liked Beryl well enough, but was far too cowed by his mother to do anything about it. And Beryl, being a fool of a caliber to put all of you to shame— and that is saying something, believe me— took to crying herself to sleep every night, wishing for what she thought might be. And THAT is what eventually attracted the attention of a unicorn." The word elicited giggles and various exited noises; Auntie waited for them to cease.

"The unicorn walked into Beryl's dreams, as unicorns do, got to know Beryl, and found out what was wrong. And then he did something unusual: He decided to find out what Oak thought about the situation." Auntie picked up a stick and stirred the fire.

29

"You shouldn't think there was any nobility in the unicorn's motives; unicorns are incredibly selfish creatures. But this unicorn was very, very old, and knew more than a little about women. He could have easily convinced Beryl to run away with him, but he also knew that the ghost of her love for Oak would come to haunt him, and he would be better off if he could kill it quickly. And if, instead of killing her love, the two idiots ended up together, well, he could find another girl, and he would get a good laugh out of it all."

"But what about Amber?" one of the girls asked, and the gallery once again dealt with the interruption while Auntie waited.

"The unicorn walked into Oak's dreams, learned how much the boy's brain resembled his namesake, and deduced the source of the problem. And then the unicorn paid Amber a visit. And then the unicorn went back to Oak, and told him that Beryl loved him, and that he should do something about it, and he went back to Beryl, and told her that Oak was very interested and that things were certain to work out well. And in the morning, Amber had vanished." The gallery gasped and gaped and giggled; Auntie took another pull from her bottle. And then one more for good measure.

The girls had questions. "She left with the unicorn? Why?" one asked. "But... she wasn't a virgin!" another complained. Auntie rolled her eyes.

"Unicorns don't give two figs about virginity," Auntie said. "They like girls who are smart and brave and interesting and a little bit crazy, and girls like that don't stay virgins very long."

"But wasn't Amber old?" another asked, and Auntie shook her head.

"That was part of the deal," Auntie said. "When the unicorn walked into Amber's dream, he gave her dream shape the appearance Amber would have had when she was nineteen if she had lived on the back of a unicorn under the stars. And he let Amber look at that appearance in a dream mirror, and he promised her that if she came with him, he could make her back into what she saw in the mirror. Among other things."

"Like what?" several voices chorused.

"He said he would teach her to ride, and to fight, and to hunt, and that he would show her more of the wide world than she had ever dreamed of seeing. And he was as good as his word." Auntie swept her eyes over the eager faces of her audience. "She was very, very lucky in that, by the way. Most unicorns never bother to learn how to care for their servants, and the women who run off with them usually don't live more than a few weeks. Keep that in mind, when you start thinking about being a unicorn rider."

There were rumbles of dismay and disbelief at that, and Auntie waited for them to die down before she continued. "But as I said, Amber was lucky. She aged backward, and learned, and became quite formidable. She loved the life, even though it was very hard. But she wouldn't let go of her anger. And one day, after they had been caught in the rain, and Amber had spent the entire afternoon complaining, the unicorn had had enough. That night, he walked into Amber's dreams and told her most people only got one chance at life, and she had had two. The first had been spoiled by mischance, and she had now wasted the second by being angry. Amber tried to plead with him, but he would have none of it. He said he was leaving, wished her well, and said that he hoped she would find a third chance, and make better use of it. And when Amber woke up in the morning, he was gone."

Auntie took another pull from her bottle, and the girls erupted into outrage and bewilderment. Auntie let them stew for a while, then said, "Of course I know what happened next. But that is another story, and it doesn't have a unicorn in it, and it is time for you to go home." The girls grumbled, but gathered themselves and began the walk back to village.

Auntie doused the fire, and carried the remaining stew back into her house. She closed the door behind her, and looked up at the bow, and the quiver, and the short sword hanging above her bed, and she smiled. She had not been Amber for a very, very long time.

==)»> «<(==

September, 2019 : This one was conceived and written in a single day, give or take a few tweaks. I was trying to put this collection together, knew something was missing, but didn't know quite what. This story made the tone of the whole a little less dark, and also gave this book its title.

Is the unicorn of this story Fiddler, again? Probably.

The Oakbridge Oak

The village of Oakbridge consists of a bridge, an inn, and a dozen-odd cottages. The whole is enclosed in a circle of enormous standing stones. The circle is split by the river, and the northern half is occupied by the village; the southern half is taken up by an unkempt grove of ancient oak trees. The villagers gather dead wood in the oak grove, and cut back the brush from time to time, but never touch a living tree, and react with hostility to anyone who suggests such a thing.

Zhanh arrived in Oakbridge from the east shortly before the sun set. He was thirsty and out of breath; there was a storm brewing on the western horizon, and he had maintained a much more than comfortable pace for many miles in the now-realized hope of getting under a roof before the rain came. He decided to splurge on a private room, and a bath, and the irony of paying to bathe after spending several hours striving to avoid being rained on was not lost on him. He ate well and was sound asleep before the storm finally arrived. Wall-rattling thunder jolted Zhanh out of a sound sleep; he pulled the pillow over his head and gnashed his teeth until the celestial bombardment finally abated.

The mood in the inn was decidedly gloomy when Zhanh breakfasted the following morning. When the moment seemed right, he asked the landlord what was wrong, and the man scowled at him, then replied, "Mother Tree was struck by lightning last night. She's dying."

"She went out in the storm?" Zhanh asked, and the landlord snorted.

"Mother TREE. The biggest and oldest tree in the grove across the river. You'll see for yourself, if you go south this morning."

"Ah." Zhanh said, and nodded. He finished his breakfast, paid his bill, gathered his goods, and started walking. He saw the tree as soon as he was off of the bridge; it was an enormous old oak, nearly twice the size of any of the others in the grove. Its main trunk had been split nearly to ground level; the weight of the branches was causing the wound to yawn precariously. Zhanh set down his pack and climbed carefully into the tree to examine the damage, then went back across the river and into the inn.

"I think I can save your tree," Zhanh told the landlord.

The landlord looked at him skeptically. "Can you, now?"

Zhanh smiled. "You can do ANYTHING if you have enough time, energy, money, and knowledge." The landlord's scowl deepened at the word "money", but Zhanh continued. "Money or materials. I have time, energy, and knowledge, but I'll need a place to sleep and food. And rope, at least a thousand feet of it. And a cart load of shovel handles."

"Shovel handles?"

"Strong pieces of wood about that size and shape."

"And that's all? What's in it for you?"

Zhanh smiled. "I'm not sure. Maybe I'm tired of walking all day, and want a few days off of the road. Mostly, I can. And the tree is beautiful, and I don't want to see it die."

The landlord nodded. "I'll see what I can do."

"I'll be at the tree," Zhanh answered, and went back outside.

Zhanh knew the job before him was huge; first he had to bind the sections of the tree together so that they would support each other against the wind, because if either section fell, the tree was doomed. Then he had to carefully remove the splintered wood so that the two sections would mate cleanly when they were drawn together. And THEN he had to actually draw the two sections together, and finally he had to use magic to heal the torn wood. He wondered how much magic it would take; he was certain it would be everything he had for several days.

He wondered if the village would be able to gather the necessary rope and wood, and how long it would take to gather it. He hoped they would succeed; his effort was doomed otherwise. But that was out of his hands, so he climbed into the tree and began scraping away splintered wood.

The rope and the wood arrived in dribs and drabs, first from the village itself, and then from outlying farms, as the word spread that Mother Tree was injured and in need of help. Wagons rolled up bearing varying amounts of rope and wood, and spectators to see the crazy elf with the strange accent. Zhanh first applied several loops of stout rope at a point midway up the tree, and then began adding a series of Beggar's Windlasses at regular intervals as the materials became available.

Just before sunset an old woman called to Zhanh from the base of the tree. "Let it die, Fool!" she shouted. "Can't you see that its time has come?"

Zhanh looked down at the woman and decided he was done for the day; he began to climb down. "I don't think so," he said as he jumped to the ground. "There is too much life left in her, and she is too beautiful, to let her die without a fight."

The old woman swung her crutch feebly at Zhanh, and nearly fell over in the process. "You're an idiot," she said. "No good will come of this."

Zhanh shrugged. "I will do what I will do," he said. "Can I escort you back to the village?"

The old woman spat. "I don't live in the village. Be off with you." Zhanh bowed to her, then gathered his tools and crossed the bridge back to the village.

The next morning Zhanh located the village blacksmith and borrowed a hoe, which he then honed until its edges were razor sharp. He then returned to the tree and continued work, climbing and scraping splinters, honing his tools as necessary, and adding more Beggar's Windlasses as he had material.

As the sun was setting the second day, the old woman again appeared at the foot of the tree and reviled Zhanh as he climbed down, and again he disagreed with her politely and returned to the village.

This pattern continued for three more days, as Zhanh climbed and scraped and honed and knotted. Each evening at sunset the old woman appeared and cursed at him, and each time Zhanh respectfully disagreed.

On the sixth day Zhanh stopped scraping splinters and began to draw the tree back together, slowly tightening each windlass in turn as he climbed up and down the tree. A crowd gathered as word spread that he was "closing the tree", and a few of the younger men even climbed into the tree to help the process along, though they left the highest work for Zhanh. By sunset the windlasses were all bowstring tight, and the tree looked much as it had before the lightning strike— except, of course, for the occasional patches of white wood along the line of the break. There was a round of applause as Zhanh stepped to the ground, and he smiled and bowed. He let the crowd sweep him across the bridge and into the tavern, and he spent the evening drinking free beer. He told anyone who would listen that the job was less than half done, that it would take a long time and a great deal of magic to actually heal the tree, but no one wanted to hear that.

Later, Zhanh made his unsteady way though the darkness to the tree and spent an hour casting the first of a long series of healing spells. When he finished, he found the old woman standing there, watching him in the darkness. She did not seem quite so frail as she had previously. "You may not be quite the fool that I took you for," she said quietly.

"Thank you for that," Zhanh answered.

For the next several days Zhanh rose early, cast a round of spells, and then rested while his energy returned. Since he spent three or four times as much time resting as he did working, the townsfolk began to wonder if he was working at all. The innkeeper moved Zhanh out of his private room and onto the common room floor, and it was clear that many felt he did not even deserve that. The small gifts of food that had appeared regularly when Zhanh was obviously working hard disappeared, and Zhanh found himself living on water, occasional bread, and an increasingly grudging helping of the daily stew.

The old woman continued to appear every day at sunset, and she at least seemed to appreciate Zhanh's efforts. She also seemed to be less decrepit as each day passed, and the day came when she was no longer leaning on a crutch, but instead carried a large bowl of cold vegetable stew, which Zhanh ate happily.

The healing took twenty-three days, with Zhanh pouring all of the magic he had into the tree four times every day. After the fifteenth day the innkeeper chased Zhanh out of the common room, and he took to sleeping at the base of the tree. The old woman, who looked less old and more spry every day, took to bringing Zhanh cold vegetable stew twice a day.

Finally, in the late afternoon of the twenty-ninth day that Zhanh had been in the village, the healing was finished. Zhanh sat on a branch for a while and looked at the village and the surrounding countryside, and then began to climb down, releasing each windlass and dropping the pieces to the ground as he went. The woman was waiting for him at the base of the tree. She offered Zhanh yet another bowl of stew, and he realized that she now stood straight and tall, and no longer seemed old at all. She was not young, but she was almost painfully beautiful. Zhanh concentrated on his stew so that he would not stare.

"What will you do now?" the woman asked quietly. "Will you tell them that you are finished, and that they can come and get their rope?"

Zhanh met the woman's eyes. "I don't think so. They'll figure it out soon enough, and I think that I have had enough of them. I've been in one place too long; there is a grove of trees down the road to the south that I think I can reach before nightfall."

The woman nodded. "Why did you continue, after the people gave up on you?"

Zhanh shrugged. "I didn't do it for them. The tree is beautiful, and I didn't think it was ready to die. In spite of someone's protests to the contrary."

The woman smiled. "I was in a great deal of pain in those days, and I wanted it to stop. I am glad that you ignored me." She took a pendant from around her neck, and offered it to Zhanh. "This is for you," she said. "It will let my sisters, all of them, wood and water and mountain, know that you are a friend."

Zhanh took the pendant; it was an acorn tightly caged in silver wire, and strung on a leather thong. He clutched it tightly in his hand. "My lady... I have not done what I have done for hope of reward, but only for love of beauty. But this... I cannot express my gratitude."

The woman shrugged. "You have given me my life; this is but a token."

Zhanh finished his stew, gave the woman her bowl, and stood. "Fare well is not meaningful to one such as you, is it? Joy, long life, and more joy to you."

The woman smiled. "And to you, Zhanh Redcap, and to you." The woman's soft smile took on a hint of deviltry. "But truly, the day is nearly gone, and you have not yet been a guest in MY home." She offered him her hand. "Take my hospitality, and meet the road at dawn."

Zhanh smiled and took the proffered hand. "I would like that."

==)»> «<(==

August, 2012: This story was conceived as a poem while I was driving from Maryland to Illinois in December of 2011. I never managed to make the poem work, but was able to hammer the concept into a story. It is almost certainly the sweetest story I have ever written, as evidenced by the fact that a friend in Australia read it to his young children as a bedtime story. Given the amount of mayhem that lurks in my portfolio, I am absolutely charmed by this.

Jasper's Journey

Jasper had no grand plans when he set out. He wanted to see the world, and he wanted to bed as many women as he could. To that end, he took a job as a caravan guard, because he was competent (and a bit) with sword, shield, spear, and bow, and he brought along his grandfather's lute, because he had already learned that a well delivered song tended to make the drinks cheap and the women easy.

Early in his career, he chanced upon a minor magic item, a strip of cloth that cleaned itself of any dirt or stain, and repaired itself when damaged. It was about four feet long and one inch wide, was bright white, and had quarter inch transverse stripes at one inch intervals along its length. It was mostly useless, but Jasper took to wearing it as a headband, to keep his hair out of his eyes.

There came a night when Jasper was trying to impress a particularly attractive barmaid. He told the girl that his headband was an heirloom from his great, great grandfather (who was also named Jasper), and who had been an adventurer of some note, once upon a time. And then Jasper sang a song he had learned many miles away, that he had adapted to just this purpose. It was an old hero story, but Jasper substituted in his own name, and included a reference to the red and white headband.

The song was successful; the girl ended up in Jasper's bed, and the next night the patrons of the bar asked him to sing the song again (twice!). Jasper was encouraged by this, and started adapting other songs the same way; he even wrote a few of his own. Whenever it was possible, though, he changed the story so that Jasper the Sly (as he called his fictitious ancestor) won the day through cleverness rather than strength of arms.

Over time, Jasper found that he was making more money with his lute than with his sword; he found he could afford to simply travel with the caravans (they were always glad of his company) rather than hiring on as a guard (which saved him from standing overnight watches). He was always able to afford a private room (and often a very good one) at every inn he stayed at. And he found that female companionship was almost embarrassingly easy to come by (so much so that, like his fictitious ancestor, he often had to leave town in a hurry to avoid irate husbands and fathers). His repertoire of "Jasper" songs grew.

After some years, Jasper started to notice that other performers were playing the Jasper songs, though they did not claim Jasper the Sly as an ancestor. Jasper also noticed that people were beginning to wear copies of his headband as good luck charms. And sometime after that, he noticed that the red and white patterned charms had moved from being only headbands, but also armbands, and even medallions. He was baffled, but gratified, and his life was as easy as he chose it to be.

One day, he made an offhand comment, while performing, that it was his birthday, and someone in the audience asked him how old he was. He blinked, then answered that he was too drunk to count that high, and went on with the show. Later that night, when he was alone in his room, he stared into the mirror and tried to answer the question.

Calendars change across borders, and Jasper had not been home in a long, long time. It had been so many years between the time he had left home, and the time his grandfather's lute had been smashed in a bar fight. He had carried the replacement for so many years, and then lost it in a shipwreck; he had traveled with that short fellow for a few years... Was he really 63 years old? But he LOOKED 30-something. He felt... Well, he felt great. He went through the calculations again, and got the same result. He MIGHT have been as young as 61, or as old as 68, but still...

There was a knock at the door. Jasper answered it cautiously, and found himself facing a handsome, 30-ish man of average height.

"We were wondering when you would figure it out," the visitor said. "Taking bets, actually, but that is what we do. May I come in?"

Jasper did not open the door. "Figured what out?"

"Your age. Do let me in, Jasper. You do NOT want to discuss this in the hallway." Jasper scowled, but opened the door. The stranger came in and seated himself in the only chair; Jasper sat down on the bed facing him.

"You are quite the success story, Jasper," the stranger said. "Without the least bit of planning on your part, you have managed to become someone whom the peasants and livestock invoke for luck. Of course, that is really the only way to do it; one simply can NOT become a trickster god by setting out to become one. Rather defeats the whole point."

Jasper gaped. "What are you talking about?"

"Apotheosis, Jasper. You haven't aged, in fact you have aged backwards a bit. And you won't. You have become a member in good standing of the Brotherhood of Tricksters. And because, as a matter of enlightened self interest, we operate as a cooperative, all you have to do from now on is sit back and reap the benefits." Jasper simply goggled as the stranger continued. "Our policy is that any worship of any trickster is shared out among all tricksters. Once you have passed the threshold of recognition, once the Brotherhood acknowledges you, you just have to get on with enjoying the meta-life. And since, being liars and thieves, we get to count a piece of every commercial transaction, to say nothing of pretty much anything any lawyer ever does, there is quite a bit to collect."

"I am NOT a god," Jasper said firmly.

"Oh, but you are, Jasper. How long has it been since you have played to an audience that did not include at least one person wearing your token? More than a decade. Of course, they aren't really invoking the musician who is in front of them, they are invoking the Jasper whom you invented, and gave your name to. But it all works out. Besides, we had to draft SOMEONE to absorb the worship you were generating, and you were the obvious choice."

Jasper scowled again. "Assuming I believe this, what does it mean? What now?"

The stranger smiled. "I take you on a tour of a slightly larger reality than you are used to, and then you make your own decisions."

"Fine," Jasper growled. "But I'm taking my lute."

"Of course you are."

==)»> «<(==

February, 2012: A friend of mine wrote an article on player character apotheosis for a gaming magazine, and then introduced apotheosis as a theme to his ongoing RPG campaign. His players were indifferent. I sat in on a session, then looked up and read the article. My muse awakened from her chronic slumber, and this story resulted.

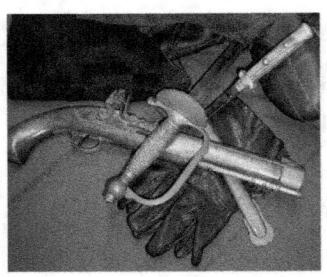

About the Author

P.D. Haynie, known as "Paul" to his face, claims to be a human being by Robert A. Heinlein's definition. In addition to being a writer, he has by turns described himself as a wastrel, a dilettante, an errantrist, an ethicist, a curmudgeon, a game freak, a math head, a history buff, a fan of science fiction and fantasy, a reluctant pagan, and a low-rent yachtsman.

Paul lives in Waukegan, Illinois, with his wife Julia and an embarrassing number of disturbingly personalized plush toys. He is currently vacillating between careers as a full time writer and a poverty-stricken, homeless wretch. He has not actually gone by "P.D." in the real world since shortly after he learned to talk.

Also by P.D. Haynie

Rose is a newly-minted sorceress with problems. She's falling in love with a ghost, she's turning into a dragon, and she REALLY needs to get her hands on a magical dagger that's lost in the mud 500 miles from nowhere under 2000 fathoms of ocean.

"Fiddler Rose" is a love story, an epic quest, and a conversation. It demonstrates that love doesn't need to be explicit to engage your heart, and that horror doesn't need to be graphic to invade your dreams.

Fiddler's Rose

Available in print from Amazon.com, and as an e-book from most e-book vendors.

E-mail spiralpathpublications@.gmail.com for updates!